Dinosaur on Shabbat

To my father, Sam Levin,
of blessed memory,
who found humor
in every situation. —DLR

Dinosaur on Shabbat

Diane Levin Rauchwerger

pictures by Jason Wolff

KAR-BEN
PUBLISHING

There's a dino knocking at my door,
"Shalom," he says to me.

"The sun is low, Shabbat is near,"
he cries impatiently.

He helps to set
the table,
And drags in all
the chairs.

He's had a bath, his shirt is clean.
He's ready for the prayers.

He helps to light the candles,
And I tell him not to peek,
When he covers up his eyes,
He pretends it's hide-and-seek.

The kiddush cup soon overflows
When Dino pours the wine.

Our beautiful white tablecloth
Now has a new design.

He reaches for the challah.
I tell him, "Be polite"

"You need to say the blessing,
Before you take a bite."

Next day he comes to synagogue
To hear the Torah read,

But falls asleep across my lap —
He thinks that I'm his bed.

So when I want to take a nap
Late that afternoon.
He's ready for a Shabbat walk.
I say, "Not yet, but soon."

And as we make Havdalah
He creates a mighty breeze
When he opens up the spice box,
The nutmeg makes him sneeze.

He dips the candle in the wine.
He loves to hear it sizzle.
He sings "Shavua Tov" off key.
It makes me want to giggle.

And when Shabbat is over
Dino leaves without a fuss.
But I know next Friday he'll be back
To share Shabbat with us.

Shabbat (the Jewish Sabbath) begins at sundown each Friday night. At home, Shabbat is welcomed with the lighting of candles. Prayers are recited over wine (kiddush), and challah (braided bread), and families share a festive meal. On Saturday at the synagogue, prayers are sung and a portion of the Torah (first five books of the Bible) is read. The peacefulness of the day continues until Saturday night. When it is dark enough to see three stars, it is time for Havdalah, the ceremony that ends Shabbat. Just as candles are lit to welcome Shabbat, a braided candle is lit to say goodbye. Family members sip some wine, smell sweet spices and wish each other "shavua tov," a good week.

Text copyright © 2006 by Diane Levin Rauchwerger
Illustrations copyright © 2006 by Jason Wolff

KAR-BEN Publishing
A division of Lerner Publishing Group, Inc.
241 First Avenue North
Minneapolis, MN 55401 U.S.A.
800-4KARBEN

Website address: www.karben.com

Library of Congress Cataloging-in-Publication Data

Rauchwerger, Diane Levin.
    Dinosaur on Shabbat / Diane Levin Rauchwerger : illustrated by Jason wolff.
        p.   cm.
    "An excited dinosaur comes to a young boy's house to join him in celebrating Shabbat."
    ISBN: 978-1-58013-159-9 (lib. bldg. : alk. paper)
    1. Sabbath—Fiction. 2. Dinosaurs—Fiction. 3. Stories in rhyme.
I. Wolff, Jason., ill. II. title.
PZ8.3.R2323Dio 2006
[E]—dc22   2005003703

Manufactured in the United States of America
1 – CG – 6/24/13

101320.3K2